MW01104037

Time of the Thunderbird

Time of the Thunderbird

Diane Silvey
Illustrated by John Mantha

DUNDURN PRESS
TORONTO

Copyright © Diane Silvey, 2008
Illustrations copyright © John Mantha, 2008

All rights reserved. No part of this publication may be reproduced, stored in a retrieval system, or transmitted in any form or by any means, electronic, mechanical, photocopying, recording, or otherwise (except for brief passages for purposes of review) without the prior permission of Dundurn Press. Permission to photocopy should be requested from Access Copyright.

Editor: Michael Carroll
Designer: Courtney Horner
Printer: Webcom

Library and Archives Canada Cataloguing in Publication

Silvey, Diane -
    Time of the thunderbird / Diane Silvey ; illustrated by John Mantha.

Includes glossary.
ISBN 978-1-55002-792-1

    I. Mantha, John II. Title.

PS8587.I278T45 2008   jC813'.54   C2008-900702-6

1   2   3   4   5   12   11   10   09   08

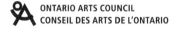

We acknowledge the support of the **Canada Council for the Arts** and the **Ontario Arts Council** for our publishing program. We also acknowledge the financial support of the **Government of Canada** through the **Book Publishing Industry Development Program** and **The Association for the Export of Canadian Books**, and the **Government of Ontario** through the **Ontario Book Publishers Tax Credit program** and the **Ontario Media Development Corporation**.

Care has been taken to trace the ownership of copyright material used in this book. The author and the publisher welcome any information enabling them to rectify any references or credits in subsequent editions.

J. Kirk Howard, President

Printed and bound in Canada
www.dundurn.com

Dundurn Press	Gazelle Book Services Limited	Dundurn Press
3 Church Street, Suite 500	White Cross Mills	2250 Military Road
Toronto, Ontario, Canada	High Town, Lancaster, England	Tonawanda, NY
M5E 1M2	LA1 4XS	U.S.A. 14150

In memory of the
fifty thousand
innocent little lambs
who never made it home.

Prologue

During the Moon of the Dog Salmon, the Earth lay buried in abject darkness for a full three nights as the Moon slept. And a great evil befell the land. It spread from one village to the next, leaving all gutted and dying.

The villagers wailed for days and nights, for what had been spirited away from them was priceless beyond measure, and without its safe return the village was doomed. It was not until Evening Light of the fourth day that the Moon responded to their grief and arose from her slumber to reclaim her celestial throne once more.

> And a shaft of light shone down on the House of
>   Weq-nac-m
> Awake sang the moonbeams to one in perpetual
>   sleep
> Awake roared the tide to one who had promises
>   to keep
> And huge padded paws slowly began their descent
>   upon
> A luminous trajectory spanning between Heaven
>   and Earth.

Wolf Spirit

I slept, and while dreaming I journeyed to the edge of the world and entered the Land of Wolves. I felt my eyes drawn upward toward the ridge where the figure of a wolf stood silhouetted in black against the pure moonlight. It raised its great grizzled head and issued a long, soulful cry meant to summon one person and one person alone.

The sound reverberated off the mountain peaks, swept down into the valley, and rolled along the walls of the longhouse like a thunder ball. It seared itself into my mind like a million silvery shards of exploding ice.

Tala sat bolt upright, listening.

"What's wrong, Tala?" Kaya whispered.

"I thought I heard ..."

"What?"

"My Weq-nac-m spirit calling me," he finished as he leaped off his sleeping platform and landed on the dirt floor with a muffled whoomph. His feet had barely touched the ground before he was up and racing out the door.

"What on earth?" Kaya muttered. "Wait! Wait for me!" she called, running after him along the well-worn trail to the beach.

Tala suddenly stopped and stared at an eerie object hovering directly in front of him. It was so close that he could have reached out and touched it. On closer inspection he found it to be an orb — spherical in shape yet small and perfectly formed. A faint light glowed and ebbed in sporadic intervals at the centre of the mass, casting an ethereal bluish tinge over the surrounding darkness.

Kaya gulped. "What is it, Tala?"

"The inner spirit that lies within us all," he said, awestruck.

The light flared, then flamed again even brighter at the precise instant the core burst open to release the nebula housed within. Once shed of its casing, it mushroomed to the point of bursting whereupon it imploded, sending a million particles of light racing inward to fuse into an incandescent ball.

The transformation was almost complete as the distinct shape of a wolf began to emerge. It stood tall and proud, enveloped in a shimmering, translucent bluish-white light that surged around its body. The wolf's steely gaze met and held Tala's while it relayed a telepathic message — a summons for help. Turning away abruptly, the wolf departed, taking quick strides down to the beach. It stopped at the water's edge to look back over its shoulder for the twins. Satisfied they were following, it walked across the inlet without further ado.

The twins stood on the rocky shore, their mouths agape as they gazed in wide-eyed disbelief at the wolf's retreating figure. Their minds were hesitant to process the information their eyes had just relayed to their brains. Surely a wolf wasn't capable of walking on water, or was it?

"What now?" Kaya cried. "How can we follow it?"

"I don't know how, but I do know I'm honour-bound to go wherever my spirit brother leads," Tala said adamantly.

Kaya knew there was no use arguing with him. Once he made up his mind, there was no changing it no matter what the consequences.

Throwing caution aside, Tala boldly placed his right foot on the water and was astonished when it didn't sink. Emboldened by his initial success, he plopped his left foot alongside the first. It, too, held fast. Tala was elated at this promising turn of events and began lightly bouncing up and down on the balls of his feet, testing the water's resiliency. "Try it, Kaya."

"I'll drown. I know I will."

"The wolf won't fail us," he promised her.

Kaya put her left foot down gingerly, followed quickly by her right. Neither sank, and she giggled in delight. "I'm doing it! I'm actually standing on water!" She started to feel a warm glow deep inside her belly that crept slowly upward, filling her with a sense of euphoric empowerment.

Tala took to the slick, glassy surface of the inlet like a water strider, growing more and more emboldened at each successful run. Anxious to show off his newfound skill, he zipped around Kaya faster than a whirligig beetle and threw her completely off balance. "This is fantastic!" he cried.

"Tala, Tala!" Kaya gasped, her arms flailing like tiny windmills blown amok in a gale-force wind. "I'm going to tell Grandfather on you, Tala. Just wait and see if I don't."

But Kaya's threat only spurred her brother on to greater recklessness. He sailed right by her as if he didn't have a care in the world much less ears to hear with. His legs pumped up and down faster and faster until he built up sufficient momentum to propel himself into a slide of colossal proportions. Then, without warning, he came to a swift halt, launching a stream of water straight at his sister.

Drenched from head to toe, Kaya glared helplessly after him. "I'll make you into fish bait when I get my hands on you, Tala," she sputtered, mad as a wet hornet.

"Slide, Kaya, slide!" Tala hollered, sprinting toward her at breakneck speed. He stopped midway through the run, sending water geysering into the air. It missed her, but only by a hair's breadth.

"You'd better quit your silly antics, Tala, right this minute! Do you hear me?" Then she pointed at the wolf's disappearing figure. "Look!"

"Quick, we can't lose him," Tala shouted, taking off.

The wolf led them deep into the heart of the forest before stopping at the mouth of a small valley whereupon it vanished into thin air. Was this then to be the end of their journey, or just the beginning?

2

The Valley of the Earth Dwarfs

N ow, as it happened, the small valley that Kaya and Tala found themselves in was home to an earth dwarf named Keiwa. He was a rather well-filled-out individual all in all, so pudgy, in fact, that he was as wide as he was tall. Although his hair had turned to pepper and salt, no one could recall what age Keiwa actually was, but it was well-known that he was more ancient than the oldest cedar in the forest. In dwarf reckoning that translated into a couple of thousand years, give or take a century or so.

Keiwa had held the illustrious position of forest steward ever since he was first sent to live on *S-weya*, the Earth, entrusted with the task of planting the original cedar cones in the valley. As the years passed, he took it upon himself to teach the villagers about the many gifts afforded them by the mighty cedar — the Tree of Life. The villagers came to hold the tree in deep respect, and even though they lived in a land of plenty, they freely chose to practise conservation.

As to Keiwa's temperament, everyone knew that earth dwarfs were exceedingly grumpy, if not downright crabby. So Keiwa could be as cantankerous as the next dwarf, and doubly so if he was feeling a bit peckish.

But there was another, softer side to Keiwa that very few people ever had the great fortune to glimpse. The little ones of the village saw through his gruff exterior, for they still possessed the knack of seeing into people's hearts, and what they found in Keiwa was good. The old dwarf spent all his spare time down by the riverbank, whittling toy canoes and miniature animals for the children. On rare occasions he even turned out whistles of every size, shape, and pitch. They were always a sure hit with the children, just as anything that made a lot of noise was.

Every year at summer solstice Keiwa organized a treasure hunt. The children bubbled over with excitement on the eve of the hunt, and sleep was the last thing on their minds when they went to bed. If they finally did drift off, it was only to dream of hidden loot. As they slept, Keiwa tiptoed around the village, hiding a toy here and a toy there, always taking special care to place them in obvious spots where the children could find them under a fern, in the notch of a tree, or in the end of an old hollow log.

The sun barely peeked over the rim of the mountains before the children were up and out of the longhouse to race to the field. They scurried from here to there and back again like field mice. When they found that special something, they squealed in delight, and their tiny faces lit up like little moonbeams, which was more than ample reward for all of Keiwa's hard work throughout the year.

> Keiwa heard their silver laughter,
> laughter rife with a child's innocence,
> laughing in delighted pleasure
> at discovering each and every treasure.

Now it might be wondered what sort of an abode an earth dwarf preferred as a residence. Their tastes varied, of course, but Keiwa had taken a fancy to an unusual-looking tree. It certainly wasn't any run-of-the-mill tree, either. It was a special tree — a candelabra tree, which derived its name because of its striking resemblance to a candelabrum.

Keiwa had once seen a real candelabrum in the Great Hall of the Earth Dwarf King, not more than two centuries earlier. It was a rather ornate silver affair with six long white tapering candles.

Keiwa was amazed that such a small flame could cast such huge shadows on the Great Hall's wall. At the time he had figured the shadows were terribly distorted in some way or other, since there couldn't possibly be any other logical explanation for *his* shadow appearing broader than most.

For hours on end Keiwa had sat in the Great Hall as if mesmerized, watching the hot wax run down the sides of the candles and overflow the sconces before dripping onto the highly polished oak table with a *plunk! plunk! plunk!* until it pooled into a flat, shapeless, congealed puddle.

Keiwa had led a solitary life for as long as he could remember, and that was precisely the way he preferred it. But fortune being what it was or wasn't, he had recently found himself saddled with an unsolicited roommate — a cousin named Ewa. The lad had professed to be down on his luck of late and had pleaded with Keiwa to take him in.

Ewa turned out to be a likable enough fellow, albeit prone to gibble-gabble. And since opposites seldom attracted, Keiwa soon found his tolerance for his cousin waning rapidly. Keiwa had no use for mindless chatter. It had never been a part of his repertoire, nor was it ever likely to be.

3

Dinner for Four

After a good long hike, Tala and Kaya came to a small clearing in the middle of the forest in the Valley of the Dwarfs and happened upon the most peculiar tree they had ever laid eyes on. They craned their necks this way and that, looking like a pair of great blue herons in their attempt to get a better view of the tree's higgledy-piggledy branches.

Kaya heard a faint rustle from somewhere under the thimbleberry bushes and glanced up in time to see a frightened squirrel scamper away. She turned her head in order to speak to her brother and caught a glint of light reflecting off a pane of glass. Kaya blinked, then blinked again, wondering if her eyes were playing tricks on her. But, no, there really was a small house nestled inside the trunk of the tree.

"Tala, look!" she cried, pointing. Then, without having the courtesy to wait for an answer, she charged over and peered in the window. "Hello!" she shouted. "Anybody home?"

"No need to yell!" Keiwa snapped. "I'm old, not deaf! *Humph!* Young whippersnappers nowadays!"

"Who are you?" Tala demanded. "Better yet, where are you?"

Kaya motioned to the dark shadow looming to the left of them.

Tala nodded, indicating that he saw it, too. The shadow appeared to be of considerable girth and very much on the roly-poly side.

"Show yourself!" Tala insisted.

"Oh, my!" Keiwa said. "How rude of me. I've done it again. I simply forget that mortals are incapable of seeing me even if I'm right under their very noses. Why, my manners must appear atrocious. Please forgive me." And without even uttering an abracadabra or a hocus-pocus, he materialized right then and there, giving the twins a dreadful shock.

Ewa soon followed suit, not completely, of course, but in stages. His torso came first, followed by his limbs, and lastly his overly round head, which seemed to pop out of nowhere. One could safely assume that the process of materializing wasn't one of Ewa's strong suits.

"Welcome, welcome! Might you two by chance be Kaya and Tala? And if indeed you are, then please allow me to introduce myself, and if not, I'll introduce myself, anyway. My name is Keiwa, and this here is my cousin, Ewa, twice removed on my mother's side."

"We're the ones you speak of, and we're most honoured to make your acquaintance," the twins replied simultaneously.

"Sadly, it's been a long time since we've hosted visitors from your grandfather's village," Keiwa stated solemnly.

Tala nodded. "We've heard Grandfather speak of you and of the exploits you shared with him in days of yesteryear. I can assure you he would be the first to visit if his health permitted, but alas, as you most certainly know, time is a hard taskmaster. I fear Grandfather is unable to make such a journey nowadays."

"Was it you who sent the wolf for us?" Kaya asked.

Keiwa frowned. "No, it was the forces that awoke the wolf from its sleep, but that was some time ago, I might add."

"We lost the wolf's trail back yonder and have been searching for it ever since," Tala said apologetically.

"Well, no harm done, I suppose," Keiwa said curtly.

"How may we be of service?" Tala asked.

"We are in dire need of your assistance, but first things first," Keiwa said. "You will, of course, sup with us, then, as time permits, all will be revealed." He had always been a stickler for protocol, and tradition demanded that visitors be greeted, then fed, before all else transpired.

Keiwa escorted them into his snug but cozy home. A long cedar-bark table stood in the middle of the room. Four wooden bowls were laid out along with four wooden spoons. The most tantalizing aroma wafted throughout the room, tweaking the twins' taste buds. It was deer stew! The delectably rich smell only served to remind them of how famished they were.

"Sit, my friends," Keiwa invited.

Ewa bustled around the table, doling a hearty ladleful of stew into everyone's bowl. Tala tucked into his bowl with great gusto, but suddenly stopped and stared, his spoon halfway to his mouth. Ewa, having absolutely no concept of what full meant, was blithely scurrying around the table for the second time. He dug deep into the pot, scooped out another enormous ladle of stew, and plopped it smack into Keiwa's bowl with a loud *kerplop!*

"What on earth are you doing?" Keiwa demanded. "Are you completely addled?"

"It's extra … extra h-helping day," Ewa stammered.

"No, no, that was the day before last," Keiwa snapped. "This is double dessert day."

The twins grinned knowingly at each other, their eyes twinkling with suppressed mirth.

Keiwa winked at them in lighthearted camaraderie. "It would appear, my friends, that not only is it your good fortune to visit on extra helping day but on double dessert day, as well." He chuckled wholeheartedly.

The twins were in for a special treat that night — soopollalie, a traditional dessert made of crushed soapberries whipped into light, frothy pink foam. The texture was wonderfully creamy, and once people acquired a taste for it, they never forgot it.

Keiwa cleared his throat. The time to explain was at hand. "And now with your kind permission I'll attempt to describe the difficult situation we find ourselves mired in through no fault of our own. The people of the village in this valley are convinced that we dwarfs had a hand in the kidnapping of their children. But I can assure you we're innocent of this horrendous crime."

"If you didn't take the children, who did?" Tala asked.

Keiwa shook his head solemnly. "Perhaps it would be best if I start at the beginning, but I must warn you that the tale is long and twisted, much like the instigator of the crime."

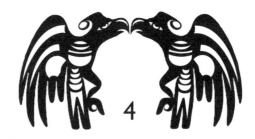

Stranger on the Shore

It was devilishly hot the day the stranger arrived. The humidity was so thick that it could have been sliced with a knife, and the air closed around a body like a fist. The villagers stayed inside during the day, not even daring to venture outside the longhouse unless it was necessary.

The last rays of the dying sun had barely sunk behind the distant horizon when the villagers poured out of the longhouse and headed to the beach. At least the sand could be counted on to be damp and the water cool and refreshing on their overheated skins.

The children raced merrily across the sand as free as birds on the wing, laughing and revelling in the joy of being young. They chased gleefully after the retreating tide only to run shrieking back as the surf roared in and captured them in a shower of deliciously wet spray.

Darting hurriedly from one tide pool to the next, the children searched for the bubbles of stranded sea foam. They scooped up the bubbles in the palms of their hands and blew them off with a hearty *poof!* Freed for one split second in time, the bubbles floated on the breeze as scintillating globules of iridescent light.

The elders' hearts filled with joy when they saw the children's exuberance. Laughter, for the moment, seized young and old alike. Yet despite the festive mood, a strong sense of foreboding settled over the crowd like a shroud. The elders began to feel uneasy, hard-pressed to recall when they had ever seen the moon such a brilliant yellow. Then a shadow passed in front of the moon, leaving its face darkened.

"Aiyee!" the villagers cried, looking at one another and wondering if someone had displeased the supernatural ones.

The eclipse soon came to an end, but the villagers' troubles were only just starting. The face of the moon had turned into a smouldering, dusky disk of fiery red that painted a crimson swath upon a sea of darkness.

The villagers didn't know whether to remain or flee. But curiosity got the best of them, and foolishly they decided to stay. It wasn't long before a small unmanned vessel was spotted directly offshore. Shortly after that, the boat was washed onto the beach by a huge roller.

A crowd of inquisitive onlookers soon assembled around the vessel. When a low moan issued from the boat, they jumped back in fear, ready to take flight at the least sign of trouble. Not hearing anything further, they crept slowly forward and peered inside the vessel where the crumpled figure of a person lay immobile beneath a white canvas tarpaulin on the floorboards.

"Is he dead?" one of the villagers wondered out loud.

As it turned out, the man was still alive, and the villagers, kind-hearted to a fault, took him in and nursed him back to health. When the stranger was well enough, he took to wandering through the village, watching, always watching. But not once did he offer to help with any of the chores.

The stranger came to be known as Qwais-Qwais. The villagers learned that he hailed from a land far away. Qwais-Qwais, it seemed, had strayed off his intended course and had ended up on the villagers' shore by mistake. Apparently, he had originally set out in search of riches. In fact, he was downright obsessed by this notion, which was quite sad, since it blinded him to the important things in life such as being part of a warm and loving community.

Naturally, he didn't find the kind of physical wealth he was looking for in the village, but his insatiable desire for it never wavered for a moment. Soon he turned his quest for treasure into a pursuit of total, unequivocal power. He was determined to be the ruler of all he saw as well as all he could not see.

As time passed, the flaws in Qwais-Qwais's character became more apparent, and the villagers began to recognize him for what he truly was, particularly when he had the audacity to demand that the Winter Spirit Dance be banned. As bold as a pack rat, he thought nothing of insulting a centuries-old tradition. But the final affront came when he insisted the villagers should burn their sacred dance masks.

Needless to say, his longing for absolute power was doomed to failure from the start. To the villagers, their customs and traditions were as much a part of them as breathing and couldn't be separated from them without both withering and dying.

Rather than admit defeat, Qwais-Qwais turned his attention on the children of the village, knowing full well they would be much easier to convert to his image. In order to execute his nefarious plan successfully, though, he realized he would have to remove the children from their parents. And, as everyone knows, it isn't right or natural for children to be separated from their families.

It was at this point that Qwais-Qwais approached Keiwa and the earth dwarfs. The master of falsehoods was in a state of total distress and claimed he didn't know where else to turn. He told them the children of the village were going hungry day after day, which astounded the earth dwarfs. They could scarcely believe their ears and questioned him further on the subject. But Qwais-Qwais swore it was true. The earth dwarfs assured him that they were only too willing to share all that they had and that their door was always open.

Qwais-Qwais became very agitated and insisted that the dwarfs mustn't let on that they were aware of the villagers' plight because it would cause them to lose face. This request completely stymied Keiwa and his people. If they didn't know what was causing the children to go hungry, how, they wondered, were they supposed to help?

All too quickly Qwais-Qwais had an answer for that. He told the dwarfs that the villagers had suggested that Keiwa and his people might be willing to look after the children until the village was in a better position to do so itself. The dwarfs assured Qwais-Qwais that he was correct and that they were prepared to leave that very instant to offer their services.

With perhaps too much haste, Qwais-Qwais told them they mustn't do that. Since the dwarfs were coming to the longhouse the next evening, anyway, for the dances that were to take place, it would be better instead if they took the children home with them afterward.

At first the dwarfs thought this was strange and asked Qwais-Qwais why it had been planned thus. The deceiver informed them that the villagers felt it would cause far less tears and sad goodbyes if the children departed immediately after the dances.

The next day the earth dwarfs arrived at the longhouse shortly before the dances were to begin. The village host greeted them at the door and ushered them to seats befitting their rank and station.

The longhouse was packed to the rafters. Rows of tiered bleachers ran along the east and west walls. A chief's bench rested against the south wall. On the north wall a curtain served as a portal for the dancers to enter and exit the house.

The drummers drummed on a long, hollow log, the singers warmed up their voices, and attendants busily added finishing touches to the dancers' dance regalia. Then the familiar rattle — *clack, clack, clack* — of large pecten shells striking against one another filled the room, signalling it was time for the dances to commence.

As an attendant pulled back the curtain to admit the first dancer onto the floor, however, the unthinkable happened. *Whoomph!* The middle firepit suddenly sprang to life. *Whoomph, whoomph, whoomph!* Flames shot higher and higher into the air as the fire crackled loudly, throwing hot sparks and cinders into the shadowy darkness.

This was a grave breach of protocol. To upstage the dancers in any way was simply unheard of, and the villagers gasped at the very audacity of this chicanery. Then they gaped in horror as Qwais-Qwais, in the guise of a shaman, gradually rose from the smouldering embers.

There he stood for all to see amid a ring of fire as reddish-yellow tongues of flame licked greedily at his flesh but left him unscathed.

He bent over and scooped up a handful of red-hot rocks straight out of the firepit. To everyone's surprise he popped each stone into his mouth, then tilted his head back, opened his lips slowly, and exhaled a plume of pitch-black smoke. It spiralled out through the hole in the longhouse roof, bearing with it a summons to the Dark Region. The smoke had barely dissipated before the longhouse door slammed open with an earth-shattering bang.

A bitingly cold wind swept through the longhouse, indicating the arrival of the Evil Ones. The villagers paled as if they had suddenly been cast amid a gathering of ghosts. Shivers ran unabated up and down their spines, holding them captive in their seats.

Methodically, Qwais-Qwais raised his rattle up, up, and up as he muttered one foul incantation after another. All eyes were glued upon him, but his gaze never wavered, not even for a second. He focused intently, directing all of his power onto the floor of the longhouse, willing it to drop away.

A loud boom ensued, followed by shrill screams as the floor dropped away and revealed a seemingly bottomless pit in its place. The villagers leaned forward in their seats and peered into the cavernous hole that had once been the floor. Flames leaped out of the pit and raged across the darkened void.

Qwais-Qwais's body started to shake uncontrollably as intense power surged through him. The villagers looked on in fear, wondering what he was going to do next. If he discharged his newfound power into the crowd, it would certainly kill everyone. However, Qwais-Qwais's sights were aimed at far bigger game. He concentrated all his energy on the chief's bench, willing it to rise off the floor. As he lifted his right hand upward, the bench did likewise, almost as if they were conjoined. Soon Qwais-Qwais tired of the game and left the bench to dangle precariously in mid-air.

A number of the elders and the chief were sitting on the bench. One of the ladies was deathly afraid of heights. She stared at the floor and gasped before swooning dead away. If her best friend hadn't grabbed her, she would have surely fallen.

Next, Qwais-Qwais shifted his arms to the right, and the bench

responded in kind, soaring over the tops of the bleachers and barely missing the spectators. Since Qwais-Qwais was only a rank novice in the art of levitation, his power soon dissipated, as did the spell. The bench crashed, dumping the chief and the elders unceremoniously onto the ground.

Qwais-Qwais's limbs began to tremble violently as negative ions coursed through his body. The atoms ricocheted off one another faster and faster until great balls of fire shot out of his fingertips and whizzed through the air like skyrockets. When that happened, utter pandemonium broke out and the villagers fled the longhouse in sheer terror.

The Evil Ones swept out of the house in disgust. They had come to witness the debut of a novice sorcerer, not some inept and lowly apprentice practise his cheap bag of tricks.

The fire waned and retreated to whence it had come. Plumes of dark grey smoke drifted out of the firepit, then reversed and plunged straight back to the netherworld, taking Qwais-Qwais, too, into the realm of darkness.

Qwais-Qwais's quest for shamanistic power was now a reality. Once he learned to control it, there would be no stopping him.

5

The Stolen Generation

After Keiwa told Kaya and Tala all that had preceded the disappearance of the village's children, he said, "The villagers searched high and low for their missing children and were at a loss as to where they had run off to and why. The village chief asked if anyone had actually witnessed the children fleeing from the longhouse, but the villagers shook their heads. After Qwais-Qwais's horrific performance, they had all raced out of the building as if a demon were on their heels. Quite naturally, they assumed the children had done likewise, or that they were outside somewhere playing in the field as they had done many other nights after they became bored.

"However, the chief became convinced that the children must have been kidnapped by either Qwais-Qwais or my people. But since they had all seen Qwais-Qwais disappear in a cloud of smoke, only we dwarfs remained as the logical culprits. The villagers took a vow right then and there to slay us on sight, which is why we've remained in hiding ever since. Mind you, I don't really blame them for suspecting us. On the contrary, I might have came to the same conclusion had our roles been reversed."

"But, Keiwa, why don't you just explain that Qwais-Qwais tricked you?" Kaya asked. "I'm sure you could make them see reason."

"I wish the answer was that simple, my dear, but what proof do we have of our innocence? All the evidence seems to point to us as the perpetrators. Still, when Qwais-Qwais himself arrived on our doorstep the very next day after the disappearance of the children, we were delighted, especially when he said the villagers missed their children and wanted them back immediately. He told us that it wasn't right or natural for children to be separated from their families, and we assumed that meant he was going to return them.

"Not long after that, though, we learned the sad truth. The North Wind paid us an unexpected visit one day and informed us that Qwais-Qwais hadn't returned the children, after all. His visit to us was part of an elaborate ruse to make us seem even guiltier of the kidnapping. He had told the villagers that he would try his best to convince us to let the children go. To make matters worse, we now know Qwais-Qwais is holding the children prisoner in a land far away. The North Wind told us that it almost broke his heart to listen to the little ones cry themselves to sleep every night, longing for their homes and families. Apparently, a number of the children managed to escape and attempted to find their way home."

"What happened to them?" Kaya cried.

"No one knows for certain," Keiwa answered with a lump in his throat. "I do know that Qwais-Qwais forbids the children to speak their own language, and when they're caught doing so, they're punished."

"No!" Kaya gasped.

"Yes, and worse, the children often go hungry for days at a time."

"Where are they being held prisoner?" Tala demanded.

"In the Upper Reaches of the Shamanistic World. But I have to warn you that they're well guarded by a powerful demon." Keiwa's face was now etched with deep sadness. "I would rescue them myself, but I fear I'm too old to make such a long journey nowadays, let alone do battle."

"We'll go in your place, of course," Tala said.

Keiwa's face clouded with concern. "I have to make one thing clear, though. Even if you somehow manage to rescue the children, you'll probably never make it back alive."

"Nevertheless, that's our only solution," Tala insisted.

Keiwa nodded. "Very well. We'll leave at daybreak tomorrow for the next valley. I'll introduce you to the shaman who lives there, and she may agree to help you start your journey."

"A shaman?" the twins echoed.

"You needn't worry. I can vouch for this lady personally, for she follows all of the sacred teachings."

6

The Enchanted Valley

The Enchanted Valley lay well hidden behind a dense bank of fog. The walls of thick vapour kept unwanted visitors and prying eyes out. No human had ever entered the Enchanted Valley before.

The delicate fragrance of wild roses drifted on the air, and Kaya's eyes were drawn to the flowers whose bright yellow stamens and pistils fanned out in golden sunbursts of light encircled by heart-shaped pink petals. She reached out to pick a rosebud but quickly snatched her hand back in fear.

"Don't be afraid, my child," a voice suddenly said. "For a rose has no need of thorns in this garden."

"Greetings, Xop'alitch," Keiwa said.

"Peace be with you, my brother," Xop'alitch replied. "My heart warms at your presence."

"As does mine, my sister," Keiwa returned.

Kaya found it impossible to tear her eyes away from the woman. It wasn't that she was particularly attractive. That was far from the truth, since her face was exceptionally plain. Rather, she had an inner beauty that radiated from deep inside her like the warming rays of the sun.

Xop'alitch had always been as astute as she was kind, and she now held out her hands to Kaya, who responded by placing her hands in Xop'alitch's. The instant their fingers touched an overwhelming sense of peace flowed through Kaya, a peace that many search for all their lives but sadly never find.

"Xop'alitch, the twins need your assistance to help them on their journey into the Shamanistic World, and time is of the essence," Keiwa said.

"Have you given this decision a great deal of thought?" Xop'alitch asked.

"Yes, we have," Tala said. "It remains our only solution if we're to rescue the missing children of the Valley of the Earth Dwarfs."

"Very well," Xop'alitch said. "I will assist you. Follow me."

She led them to a large spindle whorl suspended between two stout cedars. Around the mouth of the whorl a pair of Thunderbirds was carved in mirror image, giving the impression that they were chasing each other around the disk.

"This whorl will transport you to the Lower Reaches of the Shamanistic World," Xop'alitch said. "But be warned. It is crucial that you return here before the full of the next moon." She positioned them directly in front of the whorl and took a quick step back to ascertain if she had centred them properly. "Stand perfectly still! Whatever you do, don't move so much as an eyelash."

The twins stood as rigidly as two young saplings, not knowing what to expect next.

Xop'alitch removed the restraints from the whorl, allowing it to hover freely. She grasped the edge of the device with both hands and pulled downward with all her might. The whorl began to turn slowly at first, steadily picking up speed on each successive rotation as it whirled faster and faster until it was nothing more than a blur. The twins' eyes were riveted on the centre of the spinning disk.

Fear held them in its vise-like grip as they felt their bodies being gradually pulled toward the centre of the whorl. A high-pitched hum was emitted, then the whorl stopped dead, creating a powerful vacuum that sucked the twins into the opening and fired them out the other side like projectiles.

7

Resting Place of Souls

The twins fell down, down, down, crash-landing onto a hard stone floor. Kaya sat up immediately and moaned. "Are you all right?" she asked her brother.

"Yes," he wheezed. "I just have to catch my breath."

Kaya surveyed their surroundings quickly. It appeared as if they had been cast into some sort of circular chamber, the focal point of which was a spindle whorl fashioned from stone. Kaya ran her brown fingers along the wall of the chamber. Its texture felt bumpy yet smooth, and she asked herself how that was possible. She also wondered who or what had used stone for the wall. And why. The longhouse back home was made of cedar boards.

A seated human figure bowl rested regally against the wall. It was similar in design to one her uncle had carved out of soapstone.

"Where are we?" Kaya asked.

"Perhaps I might be of some assistance?" a lilting voice offered.

Kaya spun around, and Tala leaped to his feet. A small figure stood before them. Its torso was lithe and muscular, though the figure was a bit on the diminutive side. The head and wings were that of a great grey owl, but the rest of the body was definitely human. Two large facial disks encircled its small yellow eyes.

Tala took a step backward, his fingers tightening around the hilt of his knife. The owl's eyes were as keen as they were quick to spot the fear it had aroused.

"Don't be alarmed, Tala," Kaya said, not knowing for sure why she believed the owl was benign. "He wants to assist us, not harm us." She looked at the owl. "What is this place, Great One?"

"You are in the Resting Place of Souls," the great grey owl said. "A stopover, if you will, on the final journey. All roads arrive here, but none lead away. What are you searching for?"

"We're looking for the missing children of the village in the Valley of the Earth Dwarfs," Kaya answered.

"A noble mission, indeed! But your quest requires you to enter the Upper Reaches of the Shamanistic World."

"We're prepared to do so," Kaya pledged.

"Come, and I will show you the laws recorded over the archway," he said, brushing the tips of his feathers lovingly over the inscribed figures.

All of a sudden a great cacophony erupted, similar in nature to the raucous cries of a flock of seagulls squabbling over the last herring. It wasn't long before the cause of all the commotion became apparent.

The guards were trying to herd a prisoner to stand before the great grey owl. The captain of the guard was almost at his wit's end. His prisoner was the most unruly, most disagreeable human being he had ever had the misfortune to deal with. "Move, you halfling, or I'll run you through," the captain barked.

"Why, you runt," the prisoner bellowed, "you're nothing but a motley ball of scruffy feathers! I dare you to untie me. In fact, I double dare you. I could decimate the whole lot of you with one good blow!"

"Move!" the captain ordered.

"What's the matter?" the newcomer shouted. "Are you chicken? That's it, isn't it? *Cluck! Cluck!*"

"And what do we have here?" the great grey owl inquired.

"An enemy spy," the captain said. "He claims he's searching for two friends, but I seriously doubt the likes of this one has any friends. Let me run him through, sir," the captain implored as he jabbed the prisoner in the posterior.

"*Yeow!*" the captive roared. He spun around and knocked the captain's spear out of his hand. Then he bent over, lowered his head like a billy goat, and charged headfirst into the captain's plump belly.

"*Oomph!*" the captain groaned as he was catapulted backward through the air and collapsed in a pile of dust. "*Oowh!*" he moaned, doubling up in pain.

Tala sprang into action and grabbed the prisoner by the scruff of his neck. But he might as well have tried to restrain a wildcat.

"Come on, you big chicken," the prisoner taunted. "Fight like a man or a bird or whatever you are, or are you suffering from a touch of *chicken-heartedness.*"

"He's an owlian — part owl and part man," Kaya said. "Leave him alone, Y, or you'll have me to deal with."

"Owlian smowlian," Y growled. "It makes no difference to me. I'll pulverize him!"

The captain was so winded that he could scarcely draw breath, let alone stand to fight. The soldiers rushed at Y, but the great grey owl held up his mottled wing to halt the prisoner's would-be executioners. "I take it you two know this young spitfire," the great grey owl said to the twins.

"Yes," Tala said. "His name is Yaket, or Y for short. He's a trusted friend and companion. I apologize for his rowdy behaviour."

"Very well," the great grey owl said. "Any friend of yours is welcome." He motioned for the guards to stand down. "Now, Kaya and Tala, I suggest you think about continuing on your quest, as I believe time is of the essence, is it not?"

"*Humph!*" Y snorted rudely.

Kaya reached over and pinched him hard. Lately, she had to remind him of his manners quite a lot, and it wasn't as if he didn't know any better.

"*Ow!*" Y howled.

Kaya snapped her dark eyes threateningly at him. She knew what a scrapper he could be when he was riled. With the exception of food, there was nothing he loved more than a good melee.

"What is the meaning of the wiggly figures over the arch, Great One?" Tala asked.

"The meaning is quite clear, actually," the great grey owl said. "The Old Masters left a warning for anyone foolish enough to enter the Upper Reaches of the Shamanistic World. Here, I will read them to you. The first rule states you must successfully undergo four tests. If you do not, you will perish. The second rule says you must return to your world before the full of the next moon. Once the opening of the whorl fills with lunar light, it will seal automatically. If this should occur, you will be trapped for all eternity. As to the third rule, it stipulates that the keeper of the whorl cannot assist you in any way. However, I can give you a piece of advice — trust in your senses to survive."

"What's the last message?" Kaya asked.

"The final message is more of a proverb really. 'Only fools and dead men tread upon thin ice.'"

"I don't like the sound of that!" Y cried. "No, indeed!"

"*Shhh!*" Kaya whispered. "You'll anger the Great One."

"Come, it is high time you begin your journey," the great grey owl declared. He shared one last tidbit of advice before they left. "When you start on the path, you must follow it to the end. Things will not be as they seem. They may be real or imaginary."

"What should we look for?" the twins asked in unison.

"Search for the truth in all things that you do and remember to trust your senses," he said, then left the twins and Y to follow a path that led they knew not where.

8

Kaya's Spirit Quest

"*Halt!*" a guard barked.

Kaya, Tala, and Y froze in their tracks. Three heads swivelled back as one as their eyes swept upward to stare at the towering apparition before them — a Huge Warrior of Old.

"But ... but we have to follow the path or risk losing it," Tala said. "Our mission is one of life and death."

"Only those who possess a guardian spirit may pass," the warrior told them.

"I have a spirit animal!" Tala declared.

"Pass, friend," the warrior said.

"I am not of this earth," Y boasted. "A much higher power guards my footsteps."

"Pass." The warrior then peered down his nose at Kaya as if she were an insignificant gadfly. "And you, little one, do you have a spirit animal and have you completed a quest?"

"No, not yet," Kaya admitted.

"Then I am afraid you cannot pass," he said solemnly.

"But we travel as one!" Tala protested.

"It makes no difference to me what you do. No spirit animal, no entry."

"But ... but time is of the essence," Tala insisted.

"Nonetheless, the law is the law, and that, my friend, is my final word on the subject."

"Stop badgering the man, Tala," Kaya said. "Obviously, I have to perform a quest or we can't carry on. It's as simple as that. And the sooner I begin the sooner I'll be finished."

"But you haven't even undergone the proper training yet," Tala objected.

"I can do it," Kaya said. "I know I can. After all, *you* did it."

"She's right, Tala!" Y chimed in.

"Okay," Tala said. "I give up! Let's go for it." He gave his sister a quick hug, then whispered a few words of advice in her ear. "Wait until the time is right and you'll know."

"May we serve as her watchmen?" Y asked.

"Suit yourselves," the warrior said. "But you cannot interfere with any decisions she makes."

Kaya scanned their surroundings. "But where can I perform a quest around here? All the land appears to be flat and barren."

"There is a small cave nearby," the warrior said.

"Where exactly?"

"Just around the last bend in the path, you will find an opening behind the largest of the salal berry bushes."

"Thank you," Kaya said.

"Take this with you," the warrior said. "Perhaps you will find it useful." He passed a drum to Tala, who nodded in gratitude.

Kaya knelt on the ground and rooted in the bottom of her sack for the braided cedar-bark wand Keiwa had given her. "Found it!" she cried, holding it up for their inspection. A band of red ochre was wrapped tightly around one end of the sacred wand.

"Where did you get that?" the warrior demanded.

"My friend Keiwa made it for me," Kaya answered proudly.

"I take it Keiwa is not of your kind," the warrior said.

"You're right. He's an earth dwarf."

"That explains it," the warrior declared, sniffing wistfully. "I have not seen that calibre of workmanship in a long time."

It was freezing at the mouth of the cave, and Kaya's breath

hung in the air like icy smoke. She dearly wished she had had the foresight to bring her cedar-bark cape, which would have come in handy now.

A small crack in the ceiling of the cave emitted a strong ray of light that cast an eerie glow on the slimy walls.

"What do we do next?" Y asked.

"Watch and learn," Tala said. "Two, four, six, eight, ten, twelve." He counted out twelve paces exactly, no more, no less. Tala had witnessed his grandfather do the ceremony often enough and was confident he could replicate it accurately. "Kaya, sit in the bow of the canoe," he told his sister, pointing.

"Canoe? What canoe?" Kaya glanced everywhere, her eyebrows knitting together in that funny little way she had when she was perplexed. Despite her misgivings, though, she climbed aboard and took a seat in the "bow."

"Y, stand in the middle and pole," Tala ordered. "And I'll take the stern." He grasped the gunwales and jumped in.

An invisible canoe! Y wondered to himself. *What will he dream up next?* Nevertheless, he, too, hopped into Tala's canoe. *But how on earth does he expect me to pole on dry land?*

Tala held the drum up and gently rubbed it with the palm of one hand in a circular motion, activating its heartbeat. *Boom, boom, boom, boom.* When the fourth beat sounded, the ground turned to water.

As the canoe floated into a long, dank tunnel, Y's eyes widened in wonder at the incredible power of fantasy. Bone-chilling winds swept along the walls of the tunnel, churning the water up and tossing the little vessel from side to side like a cork. Then, after the waves turned from white to black, a large swell appeared out of nowhere and hit the canoe broadside.

The wave shot up and over the bow of the canoe, flinging the cold glacial runoff into Kaya's face. A fish was thrown into the boat and landed on the floor with a thump. The fish's body was covered in gelatinous slime from head to tail. Its fangs were long and needle-like, so lengthy, in fact, that when it closed its jaws, the incisors protruded.

Kaya reached down to scoop up the fish and throw it back into the water. When its razor-sharp fangs snapped viciously at her fingertips, she snatched her hand back as if scalded. Shaken, she picked up her cedar-bark wand and lightly touched the fish, which then vanished. But now the cold air had penetrated to the very marrow of her bones, and hypothermia wasn't far off. Her teeth started chattering noticeably like castanets — *click, click, click* — and her lips became deathly pale. A moment later she collapsed in a heap on the floor of the canoe and thus began her vision.

"As I lay on the floor of the canoe, I heard singing from far away. I saw strange creatures rush the canoe from all sides. The creatures held out their arms to me, offering me gifts — a talking stick, a mountain goat blanket, a raven rattle, and lastly, food. I was sorely tempted to accept their handsome gifts but remained steadfast to my convictions.

"I thought back to what Grandfather once said: 'Gifts must come from the heart, for it is the giving that makes us rich, not the taking.' I knew deep down that the gifts they offered were not truly heartfelt. As the creatures came to the realization that they could not tempt me, they quickly dissolved into the nothingness from which they had sprung.

"I saw a snowy owl soar high above the canoe. The next instant the most strikingly beautiful butterfly I had ever seen flitted by, distracting me. Its wings were of a deep amethyst colour lightly sprinkled with a thin layer of diamond dust that sparkled bewitchingly in the cave's feeble light. I felt myself fall under the butterfly's captive spell, only to feel crushed inside as I watched it move away.

"I looked into the snowy owl's eye up close. It was round and yellow like the moon and caught me in its stare. Our eyes locked and held before the owl faded away. Then the butterfly returned, fluttering enticingly by on wings of delicate gossamer. I crooked my index finger, inviting it to land."

Don't let it touch you! Tala cried silently, striking the drum sharply to break the spell the butterfly had cast over his sister. Kaya's hand

dropped mechanically to her side, and Tala's heart thudded with fear. If she accepted a swarming insect for her guardian spirit, all would be lost.

When the butterfly circled back and flew straight at Kaya, Tala wondered why she couldn't see the creature for the hideous monster it really was. The diamond-coated wings merely served as camouflage to hide the mass of wiggling white maggots that covered the creature.

Almost as if she had read her twin's thoughts, Kaya snapped out of the trance. She gazed upon the real butterfly for the very first time, and revulsion crossed her face. Kaya snatched up her wand up and held it so tight that her knuckles ached. Without being asked, she touched the creature with the wand. It let out a long, blood-curdling scream, then vanished.

The snowy owl reappeared and swooped toward Kaya. She ducked instinctively, yet knew the time had come for her to accept her guardian spirit. The owl came around for a fourth pass and flew straight at her. Kaya opened her arms wide, allowing it to glide through her. The snowy owl had seen fit to grant Kaya the rights to the song of the Spirit Owl:

> "I felt myself falling,
> and my spirit swooped beneath me
> with its wings outspread.
> I soared across the sky
> on the wings of love,
> and glided past the winds of time."

Tala struck the drum sharply four times, bringing the quest to an end. Then he reached over the gunwale and smacked the side of the canoe with the palm of his hand. The canoe rose upward, transporting them to another world, another time, another place.

9
An Invisible Nemesis

Judging by the large grin on Y's face, it was safe to assume he was dreaming of his favourite food — berry cakes dripping in wild honey. He ran his tongue across his upper lip. *Smack!* The noise jolted him awake, but now he was hungrier than when he first went to sleep.

Y began pacing, grumbling like a hungry old bear awakening at springtime. He decided it was high time the twins were up, too. After all, if he had to be awake, why shouldn't they? "Hey, sleepyheads, daylight's burning!"

Tala groaned and rolled over, pulling his blanket tightly over his head.

"Just a few more winks, Y," Kaya pleaded, snuggling back under her toasty warm blanket.

"Last one up makes breakfast," Y said, leaping to his feet.

"Why is it that you never make breakfast, Y?" Tala asked as he got to his feet with a reluctant sigh.

"I'll get the water, so you can make the tea," Y offered magnanimously.

Kaya searched the bottom of the food sack, but there was little left in the way of provisions. Barely a mouthful of dried salmon remained, along with a handful of dried kinnikinnick leaves.

"Oh, well, a piping hot cup of tea will hit the spot," Kaya said.

She glanced at her brother. "Do you think we'll come to the end of this path today?"

"I don't know, but I reckon we'll find out before the day's end," Tala replied.

As soon as Y brought them some water, they made tea, gulped it down quickly, and resumed their trip.

The trio travelled along for a good part of the day before stopping for a much-needed rest. They had barely sat down when Y spotted a large clump of blackberries. His eyes lit up as if he were already tasting the juicy berries squishing against the roof of his mouth. Before Tala and Kaya could say anything, he dashed over, plucked a bunch of berries, and wolfed them down.

"Be careful, Y," Kaya warned. "We have no way of knowing what is or isn't poisonous in this strange land."

"Berries are berries!" Y retorted, cramming another handful into his already overflowing mouth. Juice ran down his chin, trickled along his neck, and slid onto his chest, leaving a purple stain.

The twins knew they didn't have a chance of getting him to move on until he had eaten his fill and then some.

"Should we wait for him or push on?" Kaya asked.

"We can scout ahead, then return for him," Tala suggested.

Suddenly, Y let out a loud whoop. He had spotted the biggest, plumpest, juiciest berry he had ever laid eyes on. The only problem was that it was dangling at the very back of the bushes. He reached as far as his arm could stretch, but only the tips of his fingers managed to touch the berry. It swung maddeningly away from him, dancing on the end of its stem like a bouncing bauble.

The more unattainable the berry became the more Y desired it. Never one to be bested as far as food was concerned, he decided that a little pendulum action might be just the ticket to bring the berry within reach. He poked the fruit with an index finger, and it swayed tantalizingly closer. "Just a bit harder and you'll be mine," he chortled. Y jabbed it dead centre, and the delectable morsel flew up and away, plunging to the ground with a squelch. "Yiee!" he cried, leaping backward like a surprised jackrabbit.

"What is it, Y?" Kaya asked.

"Something … something brushed against my hand," he quavered.

"It was probably a leaf," Tala said. Still, he searched the bushes to make sure. "There's nothing here, Y."

"I'll bet it was a snake," Y said knowingly. "They often wind up in branches and lie in wait for unsuspecting birds and insects to eat."

Kaya shuddered, while Tala poked in the bushes with a stick, lifting the leaves to one side and peering underneath. Thinking back to the advice the great grey owl had given them — *use all your senses* — Kaya closed her eyes and listened, trying to detect the slightest sound. But not even the croak of an old bullfrog met her ears.

Y's fear soon gave way to hunger, and he forgot all about his dread of snakes. Happily, he began munching away as if he didn't have a care in the world.

"Let's go, Y," Kaya urged. "You probably just imagined it, or it was a fly or a bee that landed on your hand."

"No, I felt it, all right!" Y shot back. "Its body slithered against my skin *Yuck!*"

Tala shrugged, but Kaya gasped when she felt the clammy skin of a reptile brush her cheek.

"What's wrong?" Tala demanded.

"Nothing, uh, I just felt something touch my face." Kaya rubbed her fingers across her cheek to convince herself there was nothing there.

"I can't see anything," Tala said.

"I can't see anything, either, but I know I definitely felt something," Kaya said with a puzzled frown. Then she shrieked and leaped into the air. "It just rubbed against my arm."

"Well, I still don't see anything," Tala insisted.

"I tell you I felt something scaly rub against my skin," Kaya swore.

"But there's nothing here, Kaya," Tala said. "Take a look yourself." He wasn't even sure how he would go about fighting an invisible nemesis in the first place much less visualize it.

"Sn-n-nake!" Y stammered as something slithered up his leg.

Kaya was terrified of snakes and had been ever since she was a small child. And now here she was suddenly thrust into the midst of a living nightmare. She closed her eyes tighter, desperately trying to block out all thoughts of snakes. The moment she did the snake became clearly visible. She looked on helplessly as the snake glided through the air straight at Y.

"Look out, Y!" Kaya yelled. "Duck!"

Y scrunched down and glanced around quizzically. "There's nothing here, Kaya."

Kaya opened her eyes, and sure enough the snake was gone. Then Y let out a shrill, high-pitched scream as the snake started to wind around his leg. Kaya summoned all her courage in order to find the strength she needed to shut her eyes once more, knowing it was the only way she could help Y. The instant she closed her eyes the snake became visible once again.

"Shut your eyes, both of you!" Kaya ordered.

"Shut my eyes!" Y bellowed. "Shut my eyes? I'm about to become snake food and you want me to shut my eyes? Have you lost all your sense?"

Tala closed his eyes immediately. "I can see it!"

"Help, Tala!" Y screeched. "The coils are tightening."

Tala raised his knife, ready to strike, but hesitated at the last second, afraid that he might stab Y.

"Shut your eyes, Y!" Kaya implored. "On my brother's life, shut your eyes."

Y was at his wit's end by then and closed his eyes more in desperation than anything else. The second he did the snake became visible. He grabbed hold of the snake's head and struggled with all his strength to keep its lethal fangs at bay while trying to kill it with his knife.

Tala shut his eyes, prayed his aim would be true, and plunged his knife deep into the snake's head. The serpent writhed in agony, and its coils loosened their hold before finally going limp. Tala ripped the snake's detestable carcass off his friend and flung it over

the cliff with all his might. Then he fell to his knees, exhausted by the tension of delivering the killing blow blindly. Y, too, collapsed in a heap, moaning and gasping for air as Kaya raced over to comfort him.

Before long they were all fast asleep and snoring like a trio of hibernating bears. While they slept, unseen hands lifted them and delivered them to a hot, barren wasteland.

10

A Dinnertime Game

"*Yiee!*" Y yelped, recoiling in terror as he pointed a trembling finger.

Kaya and Tala whirled around and came face to face with a chalk-white skull. A death mask was wedged tightly between the roots of an old, gnarled tree. Emerald-green moss spilled profusely out of the nose cavity and eye sockets. The vibrant green of the moss seemed to leap out from the stark whiteness of the skull. The skull's jawbone hung grotesquely askew. There was no telling how the victim had met its demise — whether it was screaming in terror or laughing heartily was anyone's guess.

"Let's go!" Y cried.

"No wait!" Tala said. "I want to check it out first."

Y was ready to jump clear out of his skin if he was forced to remain one second longer in this weird land they had awakened in. He became aware of a strange, tingly sensation at the top of his scalp. It ran along the sides of his skull in prickly tendrils as he felt the blood slowly drain down his body.

Kaya looked at him and realized he was about to faint. "We're leaving this instant!"

Tala shrugged. He knew better than to argue with his sister when she used that tone.

Y glanced up nervously at the sky. Even the thought of being found trespassing on sacred burial grounds was enough to unravel him completely. His body became as taut as a drawn bowstring and finally snapped under the strain. He ran down the hill like a skittish deer with a wolverine hot on its trail. The twins raced after him but couldn't see him for the dust.

"Where did he go?" Tala asked.

"How should I know?" Kaya retorted.

"*Shh!* I hear something."

"What?" Kaya demanded.

"Like gasping."

"Where?"

Tala pointed. "Over there by that stand of petrified trees."

An uneasy feeling overwhelmed Kaya as she gazed at the trees. They seemed more like a troop of lifeless sentinels standing guard than they did trees. *But on guard for what?* she wondered. Then she realized they weren't alone. Someone or something was watching their every movement.

"Where are you, Y?" Tala hollered.

"Over here," came the barely audible reply.

The twins started out in the direction of Y's voice but hadn't even gone three steps before the dry, parched earth gave way beneath their feet. The thin layer of crust crumbled and cracked the way eggshells crunch at every step.

As for Y, he had taken the express route down the hill, tumbling head over heels to the very bottom and landing with a loud *kerthump!* The twins found him spread-eagled on his back, huffing as if his heart were about to give out any second.

"*Phew!*" Kaya croaked, slumping down wearily beside Y. "It's so dusty I can barely breathe."

"Never you mind, missy!" Y snapped. "A little dust never killed anyone. Here I am breathing my last, and does anyone even have the decency to ask if I'm hurt? Just wait until I'm dead and gone, then you'll be sorry. I'm spent! Completely spent! But do I even rate one iota of concern? *No!* I tell you a thousand times, no!"

"I'm sorry, Y," Kaya said contritely. "I guess we weren't being very considerate. Are you okay?"

"Never you mind, missy! It's too late to make amends now."

"I truly am sorry, Y."

"Humph!"

"Can you two try to get along?" Tala asked. "I'm going to scout around and see if I can find the path. I won't be long."

"Oh, my back," Y groaned. "It's broken. I know it is." He lurched awkwardly to his feet.

"Oomph!"

"What did you say?" Kaya asked.

Y frowned. "I didn't say anything. I heard it, too. It sounded kind of muffled."

"Get off!"

"What?" Y yelped.

"I didn't say anything," Kaya insisted. "Hush, Y! Be quiet for a change and listen."

"Get off me! And right smart, you big beluga whale, or I'll wallop you a good one."

Y lifted his right foot and peered underneath.

"The other foot, Bright Eyes!"

Y leaped into the air higher than a panic-stricken frog. A scrunched-up, tiny face glared up at him with the fiercest scowl Y could imagine. "Why, it's nothing more than a peewee-size rock," he marvelled.

"Hello, little friend," Kaya said. "What's your name?"

"I can't remember," the rock said. "What's it to you, anyway, Nosy Parker?"

"Well, we know one thing for certain," Kaya said. "You're a rock, so how does Rocky sound for a handle?"

"Say, I like that. It's got a hard edge to it."

Kaya smiled. "Then Rocky it is. Now tell me, how is it that a rock can talk?"

"I wasn't always a rock, you know. No, indeed. I was once a fisher. I mean to say, that is … I was a noble. Yes, and an exceedingly handsome one at that."

"Noble, indeed!" Y muttered. "I'll bet you a whole sand dollar he was nothing more than a warty old toad."

"As I was saying before I was so rudely interrupted," Rocky continued, rolling his eyes in Y's direction, "there I was minding my own business, unlike some I could mention, when along comes the Transformer. He sashayed around the place like he was royalty or something. You know the type — downright snooty. I realized then and there that it was my duty to bring him down a peg or two, so I graciously offered him the benefit of my advice."

"What did you say to him?" Kaya asked, dreading the answer and knowing that the Transformer was nothing like Rocky made him out to be.

"I merely stated that some people were so uppity that they walked around with their heads in the clouds all day."

Kaya wrinkled her brow. "Is that all you said to him?"

"Well, no … I added that it was a complete wonder to me how people who were so full of themselves could walk around with their noses in the air all day and not suffer perpetual nosebleeds. And presto-chango, he up and transforms me into a rock. Talk about testy!"

"Come on, Kaya, we have to go," Y urged.

Kaya rose to leave.

"Wait! You can't just walk off and leave me!" Rocky wailed.

"I'm sorry, little friend, but we have to go and find my brother," Kaya said. "He's been gone an awfully long time."

"If you leave me, I'll die. I'll simply die of loneliness."

"Oh, my," Kaya gasped. "I'll tell you what. You can come with us. Can't he, Y?"

Y scowled. "*Humph!* Not if I have anything to say about it!"

"Be kind, Y," Kaya urged.

"But I can't go with you," Rocky protested.

"Why not?"

"Because I have to wait for the Transformer to return. He's the only one with the power to release me from this spell."

"I wish you luck, little friend," Kaya said. "And once you're back to your old self, drop by our village at the head of the inlet. Visitors are always welcome at Hunechen."

Tala searched high and low for the path but had no luck. Then he noticed an unsavoury odour in the air, yet couldn't put his finger on what it was. Suddenly, the wind shifted, bringing with it the pungent aroma of decomposing skunk cabbage. The putrid stench slammed full force into Tala's nostrils, causing him to reel backward as if he had been punched in the stomach. Bile hit the back of his throat, and he slapped his cupped hand over his nose, not daring to breathe.

A deep, slurping noise came from just over the hill, and as usual curiosity got the best of Tala and he set off to investigate. He rounded the hill and spotted a small pond, but the closer he got to it the more his eyes began to tear. A thin layer of scum covered the slime-laden surface. From deep inside the pond a deep rumble rose as if it were purging its overflowing bowels. Then it spewed out a yellowish-green gaseous liquid. Bubbles of gas broke through the top layer of scum and clung there until they reached a great size. Stretched to the breaking point, they finally burst and released sulphur fumes into the air. Tala shivered despite the intense heat.

"You're late for the game!" a voice cried.

Tala spun around and gazed into the eyes of his accuser. "I am?"

"Absolutely! And you'd better not let it happen again, or I won't be so forgiving the next time. Got it?"

"Yes. Uh … have we met before?" Tala ventured.

"*Met?* Yes, we've certainly met. Otherwise why would I talk to you or you to me for that matter? What a ridiculous question. You might as well ask if birds fly south for the winter, or if fish swim upstream to spawn. Yes, my boy, we've certainly met, or I wouldn't waste my valuable time talking to you. Now would I?"

"I … I … guess so."

"Guess so! Guess so! Why don't you know so! I've no time for fools, much less dolts!"

"I … I'm sorry," Tala stammered. He wasn't sure what he was apologizing for, but he didn't want to appear rude.

"Well, no real harm done, I suppose. But see that it doesn't happen again."

"It won't," Tala promised. He wasn't totally certain, but he strongly suspected this apparition was a Slimy Wet Cedar Ogre.

"Don't just stand there staring like a long-necked shag. *Sit!*"

Tala complied immediately. He knew it was impolite to stare, yet he couldn't stop himself. The creature was a veritable giant. Spikes adorned the top of his head like a crown of thorns. He certainly fitted the description of an ogre, especially with his greyish-brown trunk and long, stringy strips of bark hanging from his upper limbs. Still, Tala thought, perhaps it wasn't an ogre, after all. It was well-known that ogres were exceedingly dim-witted, and this one certainly wasn't slow. Tala dissected the creature piece by piece with his eyes.

"Didn't anybody ever teach you it's rude to stare?"

"I … I'm sorry. I didn't mean to be impolite. I won't do it again."

"See that you don't!"

Tala gulped. "What … what are the rules of the game I'm late for?"

"*Rules!* There's no need for rules, my boy. This is strictly a friendly game between friends. *If* and *when* you should ever need to know the rules, I'll be the first to tell you. Got it?"

The ogre trembled, eager to taste his winnings. *Why, oh, why do I always have to play this stupid game first?* he asked himself. *It's simply unjust to have to wait for my dinner. Oh, well, rules are rules, I suppose.*

"Shall we begin then?" Tala asked sheepishly.

"Why, of course, my friend," the ogre gushed, then plunked a musty old trunk onto the ground, sending up a cloud of dust. The lid of the trunk was coated with a thick layer of fuzzy grey mould. The Slimy Wet Cedar Ogre reached into the trunk with his long, stringy fingers, withdrew two boxes, and plopped them in front of Tala. "And now, my friend, let's start. You may choose the box on

the left that holds 'everything' of value, or the extra-special box on the right that holds 'something of untold value.'"

Tala sat quietly and debated his choices.

"*Choose!*" the ogre screeched. "You must choose!"

"All in good time," Tala said.

"Right now! And this very instant! Do you *hear*?"

"Then I choose nothing," Tala decided.

"What do you mean *nothing*? You can't choose nothing!" The ogre was beside himself with rage.

"Why not?"

"*Why not?* I'll tell you why not! It's strictly against the *rules*! Why, it's not even open for discussion! Do you hear?"

"Well, I'm afraid my mind's made up," Tala said firmly.

"All the other players played nicely, so why can't you?" the ogre whined. "I'll tell you what I'm going to do. Because I like you, I'm going to let you have both of the boxes. Now how does that sound, my boy? But first, you have to promise you won't tell a soul about our little secret. If it ever leaked out what a softie I am, I'd be inundated with people only too eager for the chance to play the game."

Tala shook his head. "I couldn't do that, either. If I took both boxes, that would leave you with nothing, and I couldn't possibly be so unkind. And, anyway, I really do have to go."

"No, you can't go!" the ogre bellowed. "I won't let you!" He knew the rules backward, forward, and upside down. If a player didn't choose one of the boxes, he was free to leave. Previously, greed had always won out. All the other players had been only too anxious to pick one box, and even happier to take both boxes. The ogre tried to recall if it had been the last player or the one before who had been so tough and stringy. He was quite sure this one wouldn't pose the same problem.

"I'm afraid my mind's made up," Tala said, beginning to move away.

"No!" the Slimy Wet Cedar Ogre yelled, jumping up and down on the boxes and smashing them into smithereens.

Tala walked off as quickly as he could without running. He was determined to put as much distance between the ogre and himself as possible. Desperate to appear nonchalant, he attempted to whistle. He puckered his lips and blew for all he was worth, but the saliva in his mouth had dried up and nothing came out.

The Slimy Wet Cedar Ogre's eyes overflowed as gooey gobs of centuries-old pitch trickled unabated down his greyish-brown cheeks. To be forced to sit and watch his dinner stride away was more than he could bear. Even the thought of the empty larder at home as well as the few old bones left scattered about with barely a scrap of meat left on them was enough to send him into a frightful bout of renewed weeping. "What a life," he sighed. "It's getting harder and harder for an honest ogre to make a living nowadays." He hung his head in his hands and released great, wracking sobs.

Tala met up with Kaya and Y just as they were rounding the hill. "Skedaddle!" he cried. And the trio raced away as fast as their feet could fly.

II

The Upper Reaches of the Shamanistic World

The pathway soon brought Kaya, Tala, and Y to the base of a sheer cliff and abruptly ended.

"Do you think I can scale it?" Tala asked.

"Not even if you were half mountain goat and half marmot," Y quipped smartly.

"There's got to be another way in," Kaya said. "We've got to find it."

"Correct me if I'm wrong, but don't the cliffs extend equally as far in both directions?" Y questioned.

At that moment, as if by some preordained twist of fate, a section of the wall slowly opened to reveal the path ahead.

Y gulped. "You first."

The twins stepped bravely forward, determined to follow wherever the path led. It meandered this way and that with no apparent rhyme or reason, finally terminating at the edge of a small lake.

"Now what?" Y cried.

Kaya stared into the murky depths of the water, but the dance of light and shadow played havoc with her ability to discern one object from another. Nevertheless, she persevered until her eyes adjusted to the contrast and began to make out the path running along the bottom of the lake. "I've found the path!" she yelled, pointing excitedly. "It doesn't end, after all. It only takes a slight detour underwater."

"Where?" Tala and Y asked.

"Right there on the bottom of the lake," she said. "I'll show you. Keep your eyes on my finger." She traced the route in the air with her finger.

"I see it," Tala said.

Y nodded. "Me, too."

"We'd better push on," Kaya suggested. "It'll be dark soon."

Never overly partial to water, Y leaped into the lake, anyway, with the twins close behind. They playfully raced one another to an island they spotted in the lake, Tala way out in front as usual. He reached the island, took a quick look around, and couldn't believe his luck at finding the five pillars Keiwa had described to the twins before they set off on their quest. *Look for five pillars rising into the clouds,* the ancient dwarf had told them. *They are known to hold up the cloud base supporting the Upper Reaches of the Shamanistic World.*

"I've found the pillars!" Tala yelled.

"Then this is the way into the Upper Reaches of the Shamanistic World," Kaya said.

"Let's go!" Tala shouted.

They sprinted over to the pillars and shinnied up the fifth one as quickly as three bear cubs. Upon reaching the top of the column, they let go and fell headfirst into a bank of clouds. *Poof! Poof! Poof!*

"I wonder which direction we should go," Tala said as he picked tiny wisps of cottony clouds off his body.

"East!" Y decided with irritating finality. "Definitely east!"

"What do you think, Kaya?" Tala asked doubtfully.

She shrugged. "Well, we have to take one direction or the other, so it might as well be east."

It wasn't long before the trio spotted a pair of turrets rising in the distance, and they set off to investigate.

"Who would have dreamed that slogging through clouds would be such hard work?" Kaya complained.

"Only some of them are," Y said knowingly. "It's the thick, grey-shot, darkling clouds that are the worst ones to trudge through."

"I always thought clouds were supposed to be light and fluffy," Tala grumbled.

"The white puffy ones are, but even then that's only after the warm air has interacted with them to make them buoyant," Y clarified. Having spent a good portion of his childhood playing kickball with miniature thunderheads, he had become quite the expert on the density and composition of clouds.

The trio tromped through the knee-high clouds for the better part of the day before they came upon an old, decrepit fortress. The structure rose upward in tiers like a layer cake. The foundation was so massive that it easily straddled two of the larger clouds. The walls of the fortress appeared to be in total disrepair, even crumbling in spots. Yet the drawbridge seemed as sturdy as the day it was built.

"Drat the luck," Y muttered to himself, realizing they would have to find another way in. He scuttled around, searching for another means of entry. On the far side of the first turret he came to he located a small door built into the base. "I found a way in," he whispered, beckoning them forward. Y sucked in his breath and lifted the latch slowly, managing to do so without making a sound.

"Get ready, Kaya," Tala warned. "There's no telling what lies behind that door."

"*Shh!*" Y hissed. Carefully, he opened the door, flinching at every creak. When he peered around the door, he saw, to his relief, a long, gloomy hallway that appeared to be empty.

Kaya moved forward, leaving her comrades to stand guard. She flattened against the cold stone wall and sidled step by cautious step into the dark hallway. A faint noise startled her. It seemed to come from somewhere farther down. She took a deep breath, then stood as rigid as a tree trunk and listened for the slightest sound. Suddenly, she heard a *thump, thump, thump*, and froze, only to be totally overcome with embarrassment when she realized that it was her own overactive imagination that had magnified the beating of her racing heart.

Sheepishly, Kaya edged down the rest of the hall, then halted and cocked her ear. All was quiet. At the first doorway she came to

she ducked her head in and thankfully saw that the room appeared to be empty. Then the chamber exploded with the unmistakable clang of grating metal on metal — *clank, clank, clank!*

Kaya hunkered down, ready for whatever came next. The noise repeated, only more harshly. She glanced up in horror and spied the tiny fists of children flailing helplessly against the bloodstained bars of their gilded cage. "The children!" she gasped.

"Are you okay?" Y called out anxiously.

"Yes, oh, yes," Kaya said, her voice filled with jubilation. "I found them, Y!"

Tala and Y burst into the room and rushed to her side.

"But where are they?" Tala asked. "I don't see them."

"Right there!" Kaya cried. "Take a good look inside that cage. Their earthly bodies have been transformed into shades. Xop'alitch warned me of the lengths Qwais-Qwais would go to gain power, and she was right. He's cast a spell over the children, changing them into spirit shadows. For just this situation Xop'alitch gave me a special tube to house the spirits of the children until we can get them safely home." She held out the hollow white bone tube for their inspection.

Y reached up, eager to free the children from their prison, but Kaya gently laid a hand on his arm. "No, wait, Y! We mustn't rush into things. If the spirit shadows escape, they'll be lost forever. When I give you the signal, Y, open the door slowly, okay?"

Kaya signalled to Y, and he pinched the tiny latch awkwardly between his thumb and index fingers, pulling the cage door open bit by painstaking bit. Despite his careful efforts, however, the spirit shadows flew into a frenzy and slammed against the steel bars of their prison. The cage rocked and swayed wildly on the end of a chain that hung from the rafters.

Her heart aching, Kaya feared for the children's safety. She knew she had to collect their spirits immediately before they hurt themselves any more. Tiny beads of perspiration broke out across her forehead, and her palms sweated profusely as her stomach twisted into a tight knot.

Searching deep inside, Kaya marshalled the strength she needed to free the children from their prison. She placed her lips gently around one end of the tube and inhaled slowly and evenly until the spirit shadows were housed safely inside. Then, quickly, she replaced the stoppers on both ends of the tube so that no spirit shadow could escape. "Hurry!" she told Y and her brother. "We must flee from this evil place."

"Wait!" Tala warned. "What was that?"

After a flash of lightning, a deafening blast of thunder exploded in the darkness, R-U-M-B-L-I-N-G through the chamber like an earthquake.

"That was loud!" Kaya cried.

"Yaket!" an authoritative voice boomed.

"Yes, F-f-father," Y stuttered.

"Why is it that I always find you in some sort of peril or another," the Thunder God chided.

"He's on an important mission to retrieve the children's spirit shadows, My Lord," Kaya said.

"Ah, yes, the little ones from the village in the Valley of the Earth Dwarfs," the Thunder God acknowledged. "Yaket, come here," he ordered sternly.

All three comrades stepped bravely forward. Y wasn't afraid of his father. He knew the Thunder God doted on him. Even so, all the noise his father made kept Y on edge. He never knew from one minute to the next when a loud *kaboom* was in the works. The Thunder God's wrath could be quite scary. Once, when Y's father was only a little bit mad over something or other, he had let loose with a hearty boom and had flattened a whole forest.

"You have completed the first three tests successfully, but the final one will be the most difficult," Y's father said. "The next few hours will find you fighting for your very lives." An unwritten law prevented the Thunder God from interfering too much in the destinies of mere mortals, including that of any adventuresome young offspring. "Take this sack of thunderbolts, my son, but be sure to use them wisely. Every bolt has to count, for tomorrow will see you embroiled in a battle to the death with a terrible demon. But bear in mind that it is imperative that once you begin the assault you cannot let up for even a minute or the battle will be lost. As to your friends, they must wait until first light to climb down from the clouds."

"Why do we have to wait until morning, My Lord?" Tala asked.

"The night belongs to the Dark Region, and it is to your advantage to wait for the light of day," the Thunder God counselled.

"What else can you tell us, My Lord?" Kaya asked.

"I cannot reveal any details of the battle. I can, however, warn you to keep your eyes averted from the demon Yaket will fight. One glance from that beast will cause you to die an agonizing death."

"But how can we fight it if we can't look at it?" the twins asked together.

"As I said, Yaket will battle the demon. He is only half mortal, and so is immune to any spell the monster has. As for you, my children, you will have your own struggle. But do not worry. You will not be alone. A sacred one of ancient times will be your champion in combat. But I must warn you. He is extremely old and will require complete allegiance on your part." As soon as the Thunder God said this, he vanished as swiftly as he had appeared.

12

Aixos

As dawn broke, Kaya was on watch. All remained quiet, though. Not even a blade of grass moved.

"I'm starving!" Y wailed.

"Hush, Y," Tala cautioned.

When Kaya glimpsed a flicker of movement out of the corner of her eye, she crept forward and leaned precariously over the edge of their cloud to peer down at the island below.

"What's up?" Y asked.

"Shh!" Kaya whispered. "Look at the largest boulder on the island. Did either of you see it move, or am I imagining things?"

Tala kept a wary eye on the boulder.

Y rolled his eyes in disbelief. "Boulders move? Sure they do! What's next — talking grass?" He chuckled.

"There, look!" Tala cried. A long black scaly foot reached out from behind the boulder. Its claws grasped a nearby rock as the creature pulled herself erect to her full height. The monster's leathery wings shot up with a loud snap and grew taut, yet the head of the beast remained hidden from view.

As quickly as the creature's wings had unfurled, they folded back, leaving her head clearly exposed. A long red forked tongue flickered in and out of her mouth as foamy gobs of saliva congregated at the edge of her jaw, dripping to the ground in stringy wads of lathery foam. The monster's beady eyes were set in a vicious yellow glare as a guttural sound burst forth from deep inside her belly.

The very sight of this horror set the trio's knees atremble. Their worst nightmare had just been confirmed. This was Aixos, the largest and most ferocious of all sea serpents. The name of the dreaded reptile was seldom ever voiced, and even when it was, it was said only in hushed tones and behind closed doors lest the beast overhear the accuser. Y didn't stand a chance against such a demon.

Aixos's forked tongue darted in and out of her mouth, testing the air for prey. Then, suddenly, she glanced up and swivelled her head in their direction. The twins gulped and backed away quickly from the edge of the cloud. Aixos charged forward, her powerful body swaying on pigeon-toed feet. But the serpent merely stomped to the edge of the island and stared into the water, waiting, her tail thumping the ground.

The once-placid surface of the lake bubbled faster and faster until a cloud of steam shot high into the air. Slowly, Qwais-Qwais ascended out of the water, his arms upraised as he beseeched the Dark Region to send him an army. Receiving no answer, he cursed them silently. Then his attention focused on a flock of nearby cormorants perched on old fish-trap pilings along the shore. Standing rigidly, with wings outspread as they dried themselves in the sun, the birds resembled statues. Qwais-Qwais realized the cormorants would fit his needs nicely and began his spells to transform them into his personal Legion of Darkness.

Y's heart filled with dread. The task ahead was enough to test the courage of the bravest of men, never mind a scalawag like him. "All I have to do is hold the serpent off long enough for the twins to escape with the children," he said, steeling himself for the coming ordeal. All of his strict years of training suddenly came into play, and he knew he was as ready as he would ever be. He thought back to something his father once said:

> Fear, fearless, not much
> of a discrepancy

between the two, my son.
Yet the words are worlds apart.
What, after all, separates
a brave man from a coward,
or a fool from a wise man?
For that matter you must learn
to choose your battles wisely
and follow your heart in all that you do.

"I'm going down now," Y finally told the twins.

"One of us should go with you," Tala suggested.

"No. Wait until full daylight like my father said. Anyway, I'll catch up with you both soon enough." Y knew he might never see his friends again, and this saddened him as he slung his sack of thunderbolts over his shoulder and started down the pillar.

A deep rumble came from somewhere below, nearly frightening the wits out of him. He grasped the pillar and hung on for dear life, squeezing his eyes tightly shut while awaiting the end to come. But nothing happened, and he gingerly opened an eye to see if he was still in one piece. The snores of Aixos rose to greet his ears, and he sighed with relief.

Y knew he had to hurry if he was to make it off the island and over to the far shore before full daylight. He scurried down the remainder of the pillar and dashed for the lake. When he got to the edge of the island, he slid into the water without rippling its placid surface. He was midway across the lake when he felt something ram into his side. Whirling around, ready to face his attacker, he relaxed when he saw that it was only a deadhead — a partially submerged log!

As Y approached the shore, he spied an eagle perched atop an old snag. The closer he got to the shore the more agitated the raptor became. It rocked its head from side to side as its talons bit deeply into the fleshy part of the wood.

Y half staggered, half fell onto the beach. He was so cold that he could barely stand. When he finally managed to wobble to his feet, he found himself staring into the eyes of the predator. The eagle dived straight at Y, and he grasped it around the neck and hugged it close. The raptor nuzzled Y's neck while emitting barely audible sounds of joy.

"It can't get any better than this," Y declared, delighted at being reunited with his pet eagle. Any fears that remained were gone now, and he was confident that he would make his ancestors proud that day. *"Hoka hey!"* he cried.

13

Thunderbird Versus Aixos

The sun's light kissed the clouds a bright luminous white, chasing the dark tendrils of night back into the Lower Realms. As the sun rose in the sky to become a disk of molten fire, it caused Aixos to wince in pain. The beast curled into a tight ball and shoved her head beneath one wing, prepared to sleep away the detestable hours of daylight.

The twins scanned the hills from their cloud, desperately searching for Y's familiar figure. Tala finally spotted him astride his pet eagle on a cliff above the beach on the far shore. Meanwhile, below, Qwais-Qwais mustered his troops into battle readiness.

Far away, atop a rugged crag, the Ancient Blind Medicine Man waited for the morning light to increase. As he felt the warm rays of the sun caress his skin, he knew the time had come and mounted the Thunderbird.

"Up!" he commanded, and the great bird rose, his powerful wings drumming up a flurry of thunder gusts. "Fly, my faithful friend."

The Thunderbird folded his wings, leaned forward, and plunged off the cliff edge like a bolt of lightning. He soon levelled out, soaring majestically over the clouds. The Ancient Blind Medicine Man sat regally on the bird's back, rejoicing in the freedom of flight and the wind on his face. The Thunderbird glided in low over the island and gently deposited his rider on the ground before sweeping up and away.

"Let's go!" Tala cried. "I bet that's the ancient one the Thunder God spoke of." Before Kaya could say anything, he scrambled down the pillar to greet the medicine man. On many a winter's evening their grandfather had entertained them with the daring feats of long ago. And now here they were destined to become part of a new legend.

"Your presence does us honour," Tala said with reverence to the Ancient Blind Medicine Man as his sister caught up with him.

"We're at your service," Kaya pledged.

"Your honoured grandfather and I have fought many battles together," the Ancient Blind Medicine Man said. "I could not permit his loved ones to fight alone. I am no longer able to see the enemy, but I can detect his movements. Quickly, take these spears, my children, and point me in the direction of the evil one's army."

The warriors stood with their backs against the pillars, ready and waiting. As they did, the Thunderbird came in low and fast again, his strong wings churning up cloud after cloud of blinding dust. The particles swirled unmercifully around Aixos's head, coating her nostrils in grit. The serpent wheezed and snorted, scarcely able to draw breath as her lungs cried out for air. Her whip-like tail swished back and forth angrily.

The Thunderbird veered around once more and dived, lining up his target and releasing the first lightning snake from beneath one wing. The lightning snake swerved off course and shot clean through a tree stump, cleaving it in two. The stump fell to the ground where it lay smouldering.

A second lightning snake sped away, piercing deep into Aixos's foreleg like a red-hot needle slicing through warm wax. A roar of wounded rage tore out of the beast's throat, threatening to split the very heavens apart. The howl bounced off the cliffs and resounded in an ear-deafening refrain. The serpent's eyes brimmed with hatred and glowed like coals of liquid fire.

Now Y and his eagle joined the battle, but the raptor came in too fast and overshot the mark. The eagle changed direction at the last second and circled back, swooping in for another run. Aixos

reared on her haunches and hissed from deep inside her belly. Her curved claws slashed wildly in the air, trying to knock the eagle to the ground. Y hurled a thunderbolt straight at the beast's head. The monster turned her head to dodge the bolt, and it whistled by and fell uselessly to the ground.

Y flung a second thunderbolt, which spun end over end in a blur of refracted light. It hit the target, slicing deeply into the serpent's flesh. Shrill wails ripped the air from deep inside Aixos's throat. Qwais-Qwais, hearing Aixos's desperate cries, ordered his army to attack. The Legion of Darkness trudged sluggishly toward the five pillars where the twins and the Ancient Blind Medicine Man stood.

"You must obey any command I give," the medicine man told Kaya and Tala.

"You have our allegiance," the twins swore.

The medicine man dispatched two of the soldiers with one blow of his staff. The twins came under heavy attack, and Kaya knocked one soldier off his feet and wounded another. But, as soon as one fell, another was there to take his place.

Tala used his spear like a staff, wielding it in the air and cutting the soldiers down as if he were a farmer mowing through a field of ripe grain with a scythe. The onslaught was gruelling, and the twins were hard-pressed to keep up the pace. Despite their valiant efforts, they were soon steadily losing ground.

"Quickly, my children, swim for the far shore!" the medicine man ordered. "Bring the children to safety."

"We can't desert you!" they protested.

"You gave your word," he said. "Do not linger or look back."

Reluctantly, they obeyed and rushed to the water's edge. They dived in and swam like agile dolphins to the far shore.

"No!" Qwais-Qwais shrieked when he noticed Kaya and Tala leave. The evil sorcerer didn't want to be denied the pleasure of seeing the expression on old Keiwa's face when he learned that his precious twins were no longer of this world.

As Qwais-Qwais's demonic soldiers fought with the Ancient Blind Medicine Man, Y's eagle soared up and away, then coasted back, going straight into a downward spin that turned into a nosedive. At the very last moment the eagle swerved sharply, providing Y with a clear shot at Aixos. He let another bolt fly with a snap of his wrist. It rolled in a long, wide arc before faltering and plunging to the ground with a loud clatter.

Aixos reached up, aiming her claws at the eagle's underbelly. Y only had two thunderbolts left, and he knew he had to make them count. The eagle swooped, and Y released another bolt. A strong gust of wind propelled it off target like a twirling maple tree key.

"Get out of there, Y!" Tala shouted from the far shore. "The children are safe now!"

Y lightly touched his knee against the eagle's right side, and the bird responded immediately, circling back to the far shore. Before the eagle landed, Y jumped off feet first with a loud thump. "Home!" he told the eagle, and it climbed up and away, its wings beating steadily.

At the same time the Thunderbird returned, riding the thermal updrafts. He stopped, hovered, then hurtled downward like a thunderstone. Lightning flashed from the Thunderbird's eyes, and a searing white beam shot right into Aixos's face, blinding her. The serpent bellowed in agony, wounded badly by the hot, piercing radiance. The Thunderbird's wings clapped thunder as he wheeled around and plummeted once more, gathering great speed before slamming full force into Aixos, crushing her ribs. The serpent shrieked in agony as a strangled gurgle escaped her throat. Then she gave one last, violent shudder and croaked a death rattle.

Evil wasn't meant to triumph that day, but sadly the Thunderbird sacrificed his life so that the twins could save the kidnapped children. Never again would he lift off into the sky. Slain, too, was the Ancient Blind Medicine Man from whose body an incandescent brilliance of purest white now rose and sped into the heavens as straight as an arrow.

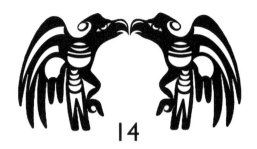

14

The Mountain Goat Riders

Kaya, Tala, and Y raced up a hill, only to come face to face with four mountain goats. The goats lowered their heads and pawed the ground in preparation for a charge. The three braced themselves, knowing they would either be gored by the goats or killed by the still-advancing Legion of Darkness, which was now close behind with Qwais-Qwais leading the way.

The goats stampeded straight at the trio, but at the last second they raced by, crashing hard into the soldiers like a battering ram. The sharp horns of the goats slashed without mercy at Qwais-Qwais's minions.

"No, you fools, attack the twins and that infernal son of the Thunder God!" Qwais-Qwais roared.

Y hurled the final thunderbolt at the would-be sorcerer, and he fell to the ground, leaving only a hint of sulphur to mark his passing. The goats then knelt before the trio.

"They want us to get on," Kaya said in amazement.

The twins scrambled onto their skittish mounts, which were eager to dash off.

"Hurry, Y, the army's preparing to attack again!" Tala yelled.

"I'm not riding on any old mountain goat," Y protested. "Why, they're plumb crazy running up and down sheer cliffs where even a demented spider wouldn't venture."

Kaya pointed at the army swarming over the ridge like a cloud of locusts. Y took one look, shivered, and leaped on one of the goats without another word. His goat was startled by his sudden move and bolted upright, almost tossing him off. Y gripped the animal's horns with both hands and held on for dear life.

The Legion of Darkness was almost upon them, so the goats thundered over the edge of the cliff, vaulting from precipice to precipice, their soft, supple foot pads clinging to the rocks like sticky pitch. Y was sure his heart would cease beating at any moment. *"H-h-help!"* he screamed, closing his eyes tightly.

The mountain goat riders rode up one cliff and down the next. Dusk was fast approaching as two bats sailed by, signalling it was time for the night creatures.

"Look!" Kaya cried. "The chamber with the spindle whorl!" She pointed downward at the Resting Place of Souls. Could the mountain goat riders outrace the full of the moon?

The goats maintained a punishing pace, sending rocks and debris flying from under their hooves on the steep shale cliffs. Night's curtain was fast descending as the goats hurried across the craggy terrain. Sparks shot from their hooves and lit up the evening sky. Then, finally, the goats came to a bone-jarring halt in front of the chamber, and the trio bounded off and sprinted for the door. Tala grabbed the door ring and yanked with all his might. The rusty hinges groaned and creaked, protesting loudly as the door inched open.

The gap was barely wide enough to squeeze through. They sucked in their breath, pulled in their stomachs, and barely managed to slip through. Once inside, they rushed to the stone spindle whorl.

"Too late, too late!" the great grey owl sang. The full moon had reached its zenith, and the mouth of the whorl was filled with lunar light, sealing the opening.

Whether by accident or design, one of the Thunder God's pet swifts escaped at precisely that moment. A bird oddly enough with crescent-shaped wings, it flew directly in front of the moon, darkening a tiny sliver.

"Look!" Tala cried as he leaped. "The whorl is open again! Jump!"

"Jump, Y, jump!" Kaya shouted.

"I'm not going in that thing," Y said, shaking his head and crossing his arms. "No, indeed, not me!"

"We have to jump," Kaya said, utterly exasperated. "It will close soon."

"No way. You go. I'll stay right here."

There was no time to reason with him. "Sorry, Y," Kaya said, snatching him by the scruff of his neck. She flung him into the opening, then somersaulted right in after him.

They hurtled through space faster and faster, with Y letting out one long squeal all the way. Tala flew out of the mouth of the wooden spindle whorl first and landed with a thud at the feet of Xop'alitch, the shaman. Y tumbled out next, hitting the ground with a thump and rolling end over end into Keiwa, the earth dwarf, almost bowling him over. Kaya was last, smacking the forest floor with a jolt and yelping in pain.

"Welcome, my children," Xop'alitch greeted.

Kaya breathed a heartfelt sigh of relief, only too glad to hand the hollow white bone tube over to Xop'alitch.

"No, my child, this is for you to do and you alone."

Kaya gulped, not sure if she could do this task by herself. Closing her eyes, she thought for a moment, summoned courage from deep inside, then removed the stoppers and blew gently and evenly into the tube. The spirit shadows floated out the other end of the tube and wafted to the ground. As soon as their feet touched the earth, the shadows changed back into children.

Xop'alitch lightly brushed a sprig of cedar across each child's tiny hands as tears welled in her soft brown eyes.

"Why are you crying, my sister?" Keiwa asked with concern. "The children are safe now."

"I have the power to heal their bloodied hands, but not their hearts," the shaman answered quietly. "Only time can do that."

15

Washing Away the Tears

Kaya, Tala, Y, Keiwa, and the rescued children started for the Valley of the Earth Dwarfs long before dawn, but it took them many hours to get within earshot of the village. As they approached, the mournful sound of wailing rose to meet their ears. A vigil had been maintained every night since the children's abduction. Tala waited for a lull before hailing the villagers.

"Yo, the village!" he shouted.

The villagers looked up, hope filling their hearts.

"Yo, the village!" the children echoed.

At that moment the parents realized their prayers had been answered, and a cry went up that hasn't been heard before or since along the entire length of the Northwest Coast. After innumerable hugs, kisses, and tears, the children finally settled down in their own beds for the night, safe in the knowledge that they were home where they belonged.

Early the next morning messengers were dispatched to the surrounding villages, inviting them to a great feast to be held in four days. The children were abuzz with excitement — they had been asked to act as hosts on the day of the feast!

Long before dawn of the day of the feast, the children assembled on the beach dressed in their finest regalia to await the arrival of their guests. The first of twenty large travelling canoes entered the bay shortly after daybreak. The two lead canoes were firmly lashed together, and a dance platform straddled the gunwales. A wolf dancer danced on the bow of the canoe as a sign of respect to the hosting village. "We have come long and far and ask permission to land in your territory," the visiting speaker requested.

"We bid you welcome and grant you permission to rest upon our shores and partake of the humble feast we have prepared for you," the oldest of the returned children piped up.

After all the guests were seated inside the longhouse, the ceremonies and speeches commenced. Little Mayuk, who hadn't spoken a word since he had been abducted, offered to lead the dance in honour of the Ancient Blind Medicine Man and the Thunderbird. The drums started to vibrate vigorously as the children entered the dance floor.

With Little Mayuk in the lead, the children glided across the floor with arms outstretched, imitating the flight of the mighty Thunderbird. As they danced, the feathers on their dance shirts fluttered freely in the breeze.

"Friends, relatives, elders, and honoured chiefs, we are gathered here today to recognize four people who have served our people well, and I ask you to bear witness to their deeds," the master of ceremonies announced.

Kaya, Tala, Y, and Keiwa stood on top of four mountain goat blankets spread on the floor of the house. Four of the smaller children came forward to bestow cedar-bark headbands on the guests of honour, then sprinkled their heads with eagle down. Next, two sets of twins strode forward, bearing gifts on beds of cedar boughs. As each recipient's name was called out, a gift was presented.

"To Yaket, who helped guard the bone tube housing the future of our nation, we present a feast bowl symbolizing the body of the house. And to Kaya, who found the strength to journey within, we freely give the tinder with which to kindle the house fires. And to Tala, who maintained balance throughout the journey, we entrust a drum, the heartbeat of the house. And to Keiwa, who had the presence of mind to reach out when help was needed, we offer a seed cone from the Tree of Life, the very foundation of our house."

Dishes laden with dried mountain goat, roast deer, and succulent duck were set before the guests on long cedar planks. There were also blackberry and blueberry cakes, and bowls of freshly peeled salmonberry and thimbleberry sprouts, steamed leaves of young stinging nettle, and camas bulbs. In addition dishes of eulachon grease were liberally interspersed between the platters for the guests to dip their food in. The grease was so rich that the guests made mention of its quality.

Four strong men then brought out a huge feast dish in the shape of a frog. It was laden with baked, smoked, and steamed clams, prawns, crabs, mussels, halibut, red snapper, and herring, as well as barbecue salmon nestled on a bed of black seaweed. At the end of the meal the children passed out finger bowls and cedar napkins.

It was a joyous occasion, a time to renew old bonds and ties, a time for celebration. And the cleansing sound of laughter soon filled the longhouse to overflowing once again.

Glossary

Aixos: The double-headed or single-headed sea serpent plays an important role in the traditional stories, rituals, and art of the First Nations of the Pacific Northwest. Aixos, in *Time of the Thunderbird*, is a single-headed sea serpent. Commonly, sea serpents are symbols of power and wealth, can transform themselves at will, and can travel across land, sea, and sky. A glance from a sea serpent can kill or petrify the unwary. It is also a creature that has power that can be transferred to individuals who are ritually prepared for it. The Thunderbird is the sea serpent's natural enemy.

Candelabrum: A large, branched candlestick holder for several candles or lamps.

Cedar: The cedars referred to in *Time of the Thunderbird* are western red cedars, a coniferous tree that is actually not a true cedar. The western red cedar, or *Thuja plicata*, is a member of the cypress family and is found in great numbers on the Northwest Coast of North America from northern California to southern Alaska. They can grow to enormous height and girth, some topping sixty metres with diameters of six metres. The western red cedar is also long-lived and can survive as long as a thousand years. The Coast Salish and other First Nations of the Pacific Northwest revere the western red cedar as the Tree of Life and make more than two dozen products from it, including baskets, bowls, boxes, whistles, floats, garments, capes, hats, canoes, houses, and even diapers. The western red cedar is the official tree of British Columbia.

Coast Salish: A collective name given to First Nations whose languages and dialects are part of the Salishan family. Today the Coast Salish, who live in British Columbia and Washington State, prefer to be called by their correct names such as Sto:lo. In British Columbia the Coast Salish are found in the Lower Fraser River Valley, on southeast Vancouver Island, and on some of the Gulf Islands. Northern Coast Salish live in the northern half of the Strait of Georgia (Bute Inlet and Johnstone Strait southward to Parksville on Vancouver Island and Roberts Creek on the mainland). Central Coast Salish live at the southern end of the Strait of Georgia, along most of the Strait of Juan de Fuca, and in the Lower Fraser Valley. Southern Coast Salish territory extends from Samish Bay in Washington State southward to the head of Puget Sound. Southwest Coast Salish territory stretches from north of the Queets River in Washington's Olympic Peninsula south to Willapa Bay and the drainages of the Queets, Quinault, and Chehalis Rivers, as well as the lower drainage of the Cowlitz River.

Cormorant: This medium to large long-necked, fish-eating, diving seabird (also often called a shag) has numerous species that are found throughout much of the world. The double-crested cormorant, the pelagic cormorant, and Brandt's cormorant are found in the Pacific Northwest.

Eagle: A symbol of power and strength among First Nations cultures in the Pacific Northwest, the eagle is frequently depicted in Coast Salish artwork, myth, and legend. Eagle down is used at special occasions such as the First Salmon Ceremony, where the down is sprinkled to acknowledge the solemnity of the event.

Kinnikinnick: This shrub is found commonly in the Pacific Northwest and is much-loved by bears, hence one of its other names — bearberry.

Longhouse: Built in rectangular shapes with their doors facing water so that warriors could survey for raiding war parties, longhouses traditionally featured large carved Welcoming figures mounted outside doorways to greet newcomers to a village. A Coast Salish longhouse mentioned by early nineteenth-century explorer Simon Fraser was described as one hundred and eighty metres long, eighteen metres broad, and five and a half metres high. Several families lived in each longhouse.

Owl: In Pacific Northwest aboriginal cultures, the owl is frequently associated with death, possibly because of its silent flight, eerie call, and nocturnal habits. Among many First Nations of the Northwest Coast, it is believed that when a person hears the call of an owl, he or she will soon die. As in other traditions around the world, the owl is also viewed as a symbol of wisdom. In British Columbia, snowy owls and great grey owls are two of many species of this carnivorous bird, which dines on everything from rodents to other birds.

Pecten Shell: Pecten is another name for the scallop whose shells are used in various Northwest Coast First Nations dances.

Seated Human Figure Bowl: The Coast Salish sculpted large bowls out of soapstone that depict a seated human figure generally holding a bowl. Animals such as frogs, owls, and snakes were often carved on the bowls. Approximately sixty of these bowls have been recovered along the Fraser River, on Vancouver Island, and on the Sechelt Peninsula. The bowls are believed to have been used by shamans in secret rituals.

Shag: See *Cormorant.*

Shaman: A First Nations medicine man or woman who has magical powers to heal the sick, foretell future events, and help warriors in time of battle. The shaman often performs public healing ceremonies that also include singing and drumming. To become a shaman a person has to undergo a rigorous process of fasting, bathing, and purification to become ritually cleansed in order to acquire a supernatural helper.

Snag: A standing dead tree or broken stump, especially a tree trunk or root embedded underwater.

Spindle Whorl: In the Pacific Northwest, particularly among the Coast Salish, making clothes and blankets by hand spinning was quite common before and after the arrival of Europeans. One hand-spinning method involves a round spindle whorl. Fashioned from stone or wood, whorls are devices with holes in the middle that are used as weights on long wooden shafts called spindles. As the shaft is twirled by hand, the whorl helps to keep the shaft turning. It also keeps the finished yarn from slipping off the shaft. Many Coast Salish spindle whorls are carved with elaborate designs that feature stylized human and animal patterns. Legend has it that as the whorl turns, the designs blur together and can hypnotize the spinner, causing a trance state that allows the spinner to imbue his or her creations with special powers.

Spirit Quest: To obtain a guardian spirit such as a wolf or an owl, people must complete a Spirit Quest. Before embarking on the quest, candidates undergo gruelling regimens of training and fasting. Individuals then seek out their guardian spirits in remote areas and have their power animals or spirits revealed to them in visions.

S-weya: Coast Salish name for the Earth.

Thunderbird: A mythological creature common to many First Nations people of North America, the Thunderbird is thought to create thunder by flapping his powerful wings while lightning flashes from his eyes when he blinks. Thunderbirds live in the mountains, are forces of good, and are the natural enemies of sea serpents and killer whales. Some people believe that Thunderbirds were inspired by California condors, which were once found as far north as Canada.

Twins: In many First Nations cultures, twins are considered a blessing and thought to have supernatural powers. Twins are often sent down rivers to greet the first salmon while singing special songs as they are thought to "sense" the arrival of the salmon before others. It is also believed that twins are able to control the weather.

Water Strider: This type of predatory insect relies on surface tension to "walk" or "skate" on top of water. Their water-repellent legs are able to generate vortices in water that carry enough backward momentum to propel the insects forward. Water striders live on the surface of ponds, slow streams, marshes, and other quiet waters. They are able to move as fast as 1.5 metres per second and are found all over the world.

Weq-nac-m: Coast Salish name for a wolf.

Whirligig Beetle: This water beetle usually lives on the surface of streams and ponds. When frightened, it will swim rapidly in circles, hence its name. The insect has divided eyes that allow it to see above and below water. Found throughout the world, the whirligig beetle's bite can cause allergic reactions in certain people.

Wolf: The wolf is a very important animal to most First Nations peoples, who attribute supernatural powers to the creature and treat it with respect and dignity. The wolf represents strength, courage, and wisdom and is associated with enhanced hunting abilities. The wolf is often maligned in story and myth, but through education, people have come to understand the crucial role wolves play in environmental disease and pest control and their contribution to the forest ecosystem. Sadly, the grey wolf or timber wolf is found in diminishing numbers in the Pacific Northwest.

Wolverine: This bulky, bear-like animal, a member of the weasel family, is an intelligent creature that often steals trap bait without getting caught, climbs trees with great speed, and sneaks up on unsuspecting prey. Wolverines are very strong and have been known to drive much larger animals such as bears and mountain lions away from their kills. They are also capable of killing moose, which are thirty-five times their weight.